Sabrina
The Teenage Witch™

Becoming a Witch

By Shelagh Canning
"SABRINA, THE TEENAGE WITCH"
Based on Characters Appearing in Archie Comics

Developed for Television by Jonathan Schmock
Pilot Episode Teleplay by Nell Scovell
Television Story by Barney Cohen & Kathryn Wallack

Simon Spotlight

Photographs by Don Cadette
Cover photograph by Bob D'Amico

 SIMON SPOTLIGHT
An imprint of Simon & Schuster Children's Publishing Division
1230 Avenue of the Americas
New York, New York 10020
™Archie Comic Publications Inc. © 1998 Viacom Productions Inc.
10 9 8 7 6 5 4 3 2
Library of Congress Catalog Card Number 97-67744
ISBN: 0-689-82123-9

W hat do you mean I'm a witch?" Sabrina cried. It was the morning of Sabrina's sixteenth birthday, and her aunts Zelda and Hilda had just delivered the news.

"I know it's a surprise," said Zelda. "But you're not alone. I'm a witch, Hilda's a witch, and your father is a witch."

"I'd really love to discuss this," Sabrina said, grabbing her jacket. "But this is my first day at a new school. The bus is picking me up in five minutes."

"Just don't make too many hand gestures," said Hilda.

When Sabrina arrived at Westbridge High, she was nervous.

I hope the kids are nice, she thought. *Hmm . . . now there's a cute guy.*

Harvey noticed Sabrina looking at him and gave her a friendly smile.

Across the hall, a classroom door opened.

"Summer's over," said Mr. Pool, the biology teacher. "Come on in."

Sabrina sat alone at one of the lab tables. She noticed that Harvey was in the same class.

"Listen up, everybody," said Mr. Pool. "Choose a lab partner and we can hop right into frog dissection."

"Hey," Harvey called to Sabrina, "want to be my—"

"I'll be your partner, Harvey," Libby interrupted as she slid into the seat next to Harvey. Libby was the most popular girl in school.

Sabrina sighed, but it wasn't long before another student introduced herself. "Hi, I'm Jenny," said the girl.

"Can I be your partner?"

Sabrina was relieved! "You sure can," she said to Jenny. "The last thing I want is to sit here alone dissecting a frog!"

"I know what it's like," Jenny said. "I was the new kid last year. Hey, let's name the frog Tad . . . Tad Pole!"

After biology lab, Sabrina headed for the girls' bathroom. Libby and her friends were there.

"May we help you, *freak*?" Libby asked Sabrina.

Sabrina looked at Libby. "I just need to wash my hands," she said. "Frog juice."

A nasty smile formed on Libby's lips. "You know, if you smell," she said, "it's not fair to blame the frog."

Sabrina was about to reply, but then decided it wasn't worth it. As she made a "forget it" gesture, a strange thing happened. Libby's hand began to scribble lipstick all over her face—and she could not do a thing about it!

Libby's friends watched in horror as her face turned into a horrible red mask. Sabrina quickly ran out.

After school, Hilda told Sabrina that there was a present from her father on the table. It was a thick, leather-bound book that looked really old.

Sabrina was disappointed. "'The Discovery of Magic'?" she said. "What's wrong with The Gap?"

Sabrina slowly thumbed through the pages and came to a picture of her father, Edward. "Happy birthday, Sabrina," said the picture. "I'm not a hologram. I'm just in a different realm."

"A different realm?" cried Sabrina. "I thought you were in Toronto!"

"Zelda! Hilda!" Edward called out. "Didn't you explain that she's a witch?"

"She doesn't believe us," Hilda answered.

Sabrina had heard enough, and slammed the book shut. "I'm going to my room," she said. "Come on, Salem."

"Can I finish my milk first?" said Salem.

Sabrina froze. "The cat just talked, didn't he?" she wailed. "That does it!"

Sabrina ran up the stairs, only to find the big book following her.

"Open me, Sabrina!" Edward called out sternly from the book. "Now!"

"No! I'm not talking to a book," said Sabrina.

But when the book began to fly around, she grabbed it before stomping off to her room.

"Honey, I know this is hard to accept," Edward said. "But you can't run away from who you are."

"I knew who I was," said Sabrina, "but everything is changing. What about Mom? Is she still in Peru?"

"Yes, she is," said Edward.

"Good, I can go live with her," said Sabrina.

"Actually, you can't," said Edward. "If you see her in the next two years, she'll turn into a ball of wax."

"You're kidding!" said Sabrina. "Why?"

"It's one way to discourage mortal-witch marriage," Edward explained. "Now, why don't you take some time to think about all this. If you need me, I'm in the index."

Sabrina closed the book and sighed.

"Okay, I've thought about it," Sabrina told her aunts. "I guess I believe I'm a witch, even though I still don't believe it."

Hilda and Zelda were delighted. Now the fun could begin!

"Start with the basics," Zelda said as she eagerly placed an orange on the table. "Now, turn the orange into an apple. Point and concentrate."

Sabrina stretched out her arm and pointed. At first

nothing happened. Suddenly the orange began to shake. Then it started to smoke. And—*poof!*—it transformed into a . . . pineapple!

"I'm not very good at this," Sabrina said.

Several dozen pineapples later, the newest witch decided to give it one last try.

"Cat into apple!" Sabrina called, pointing at Salem.

"That's quite enough for tonight," Salem shot back.

The following day at school was almost as bad as the one before. First, Jenny accidentally dropped her book bag on Sabrina's foot. Then Sabrina flunked a history quiz. And a football flew out of nowhere and hit her on the head!

It wasn't until lunchtime that things began to look up. Harvey came over to Sabrina in the cafeteria.

"Can I sit here?" he asked.

"Sure," Sabrina said. "You know Jenny, don't you?"
Harvey nodded just as Libby strolled by.

"Hi, Harvey," Libby said, ignoring Sabrina and Jenny.
"I'm having a party on Saturday. Will you be there?"

"Okay," said Harvey. "I'm not doing anything else."

"Great!" Libby said, before knocking her cup of soda all
over Sabrina.

"Oh, sorry . . . ," said Libby, walking away.

Sabrina could not believe it. "You did that on purpose!" she said.

Libby kept on walking.

"Stop!" Sabrina yelled as she pointed at Libby. "I'm talking to you!"

Suddenly the room filled with thunderclaps, and a blast of wind sent paper plates and napkins flying. A bolt of lightning shot out of Sabrina's finger and hit Libby—turning her into a pineapple! Sabrina's magic was out of control!

Not knowing what else to do, Sabrina grabbed the pineapple and ran out.

"I hate being a witch," Sabrina screamed as she burst into the kitchen and dumped the pineapple onto the table. "I turned the most popular girl in school into a pineapple! Can you fix it?"

Zelda quickly undid Sabrina's spell. Libby reappeared in a flash.

"You did something to me," Libby yelled at Sabrina as she ran out of the house. "You really are a freak, and everyone's going to know it!"

Sabrina was devastated. She was not going to make any friends at this school. Suddenly, Sabrina had a brainstorm—maybe she could turn back time!

But her aunts said no, that was one thing a witch could not do. "All you can do is appeal to the Witches' Council," said Hilda, "but they rarely grant time reversals."

"How do I get to the Council?" Sabrina asked.

"It's a million light-years away," said Zelda, "but there's a shortcut through the linen closet."

Casting his image on the wall, Zelda added, "Drell is the head honcho. He's a pigheaded, power-mad despot."

"We used to date," said Hilda. "Haven't seen him in decades."

"Not since he left her at the altar," said Zelda quietly. "Now, turn right at the towels and follow the signs."

Sabrina went as far as she could in the closet. Suddenly there was a flash of light, and the door opened. "Is this the Witches' Council?" she asked nervously.

"Yes!" said a witch. "You don't have an appointment!"

"Oh, please! This won't take long," Sabrina pleaded. "I have to turn back time."

Sabrina quickly began telling the witches about her first day of school, the pineapples, and Libby's threat. "She's not a witch, but she has the power to turn the whole school against me," she said.

The witches did not take long to make their decision. "Request denied!" Drell cried.

Back home, Sabrina told her aunts the bad news. Then she went to her room.

The following morning, Sabrina refused to go to school. "Everyone will laugh at me," she told her aunts.

But when Hilda threatened to turn her into a cat, Sabrina finally went.

After she left, Zelda convinced Hilda to persuade Drell to change his mind.

A few seconds later, Hilda barged into the Witches' Council.

"Drell!" she shrieked. "It's payback time!"

Sabrina expected the worst when she got to school. *Why didn't I ask about becoming invisible?* she thought.

Suddenly Jenny tapped her on the shoulder. "Hold my book bag a minute?" Jenny asked.

"What?" said Sabrina. "You asked me that yesterday."

"I got this bag last night," Jenny said. "Are you okay?"

Sabrina realized what must have happened. "Couldn't be better," she said, smiling slyly. "Come on, history is next, and I have a great feeling about it."

Sabrina aced the history test. As she headed for the cafeteria, a football flew toward her, but this time Sabrina whipped around and caught it.

"Great catch!" said Harvey.

Sabrina knew just what she was going to say when Harvey stopped by their table at lunch.

"Can I sit here?" he asked Sabrina and Jenny.

"Sure," said Sabrina.

"That was some catch," said Harvey.

"I was in the zone. But let's not dwell on that," Sabrina said quickly. "If you're not doing anything Saturday night, would you like to go to a movie with Jenny and me?"

"Sounds like fun," said Harvey—just as Libby walked by.

"Hi, Harvey," Libby said. "I'm having a party on Saturday night. Will you be there?"

When Harvey told her that he already had plans, Libby was furious. She tried to knock the soda off her tray, but Sabrina quickly pointed at the cup. It spun around, and soda splashed all over Libby instead!

Sabrina nearly flew home after school. "I love being a witch!" she told her aunts. "I've got to tell Salem!" she added, as she poured herself a glass of milk before running up to her room.

Picking up the cat, she said, "The teachers think I'm smart, the jocks think I'm cool, and I have a date! I'm beginning to really like this magic stuff!"

"Don't bother to thank me," said Salem, eyeing Sabrina's glass of milk. "Just share."

SWEEPSTAKES

What would you do with Sabrina's magic powers?

*You could win a visit to the set,
a $1000 savings bond, and
other magical prizes!*

GRAND PRIZE: A tour of the set of *Sabrina, The Teenage Witch* and a savings bond worth $1000 upon maturity

10 FIRST PRIZES: Sabrina's Cauldron, filled with one Sabrina, The Teenage Witch CD-ROM, one set of eight Archway Paperbacks, one set of three Simon Spotlight children's books, and one Hasbro Sabrina fashion doll

25 SECOND PRIZES: One Sabrina, The Teenage Witch CD-ROM

50 THIRD PRIZES: One Hasbro Sabrina fashion doll

100 FOURTH PRIZES: A one-year subscription to Sabrina, The Teenage Witch comic book, published by Archie Comics

Sabrina, The Teenage Witch™ Sweepstakes Official Rules:

1. No Purchase Necessary. Enter by mailing the completed Official Entry Form or by mailing on a 3" x 5" card your name, address, and daytime telephone number to Pocket Books/Sabrina, The Teenage Witch Sweepstakes, 13th Floor, 1230 Avenue of the Americas, NY, NY 10020. Entries must be received by 7/1/98. Not responsible for lost, late, damaged, stolen, illegible, mutilated, incomplete, not delivered entries, or for typographical errors in the entry form or rules. Entries are void if they are in whole or in part illegible, incomplete, or damaged. Enter as often as you wish, but each entry must be mailed separately. Winners will be selected at random from all eligible entries received in a drawing to be held on or about 7/7/98. Winners will be notified by mail.

2. Prizes: One Grand Prize: A weekend (four days/three nights) trip to Los Angeles for two people including round-trip coach airfare from the major airport nearest the winner's residence, ground transportation or car rental, meals, three nights in a hotel (one room, occupancy for two), and a tour of the set of Sabrina, The Teenage Witch (approximate retail value $3500.00) and a savings bond worth $1000 (SUS) upon maturity in 18 years. Travel accommodations are subject to availability; certain restrictions apply. 10 First Prizes: Sabrina's Cauldron, filled with one CD-ROM (a Windows 95 compatible program), one set of eight Sabrina, The Teenage Witch books published by Archway Paperbacks, one set of three Simon Spotlight children's books, and one Hasbro Sabrina fashion doll (approximate retail value $100). 25 Second Prizes: Sabrina, The Teenage Witch CD-ROM, published by Simon & Schuster Interactive (approximate retail value $30). 50 Third Prizes: Sabrina, The Teenage Witch doll (approximate retail value $17.99). 100 Fourth Prizes: a one-year subscription to Sabrina, The Teenage Witch comic book, published by Archie Comics (approximate retail value $15). The Grand Prize must be taken on the dates specified by sponsors.

3. The sweepstakes is open to legal residents of the U.S. and Canada (excluding Quebec). Prizes will be awarded to the winner's parent or legal guardian if under 18. Any minor taking a Grand Prize trip must be accompanied by a parent or legal guardian. Void in Puerto Rico and wherever prohibited or restricted by law. All federal, state, and local laws apply. Employees of Viacom International, Inc., their families living in the same household, and its subsidiaries and their affiliates and their respective agencies and participating retailers are not eligible.

4. One prize per person or household. Prizes are not transferable and may not be substituted except by sponsors, in event of prize unavailability, in which case a prize of equal or greater value will be awarded. All prizes will be awarded. The odds of winning a prize depend upon the number of eligible entries received.

5. If a winner is a Canadian resident, then he/she must correctly answer a skill-based question administered by mail.

6. All expenses on receipt and use of prize, including federal, state, and local taxes, are the sole responsibility of the winners. Winners may be required to execute and return an Affidavit of Eligibility and Release and all other legal documents that the sweepstakes sponsor may require (including a W-9 tax form) within 15 days of attempted notification or an alternate winner will be selected. Grand Prize Winner's travel companion will be required to execute a liability release prior to ticketing.

7. By accepting a prize, winners or winners' parents or legal guardians on winners' behalf agree to allow use of their names, photographs, likenesses, and entries for any advertising, promotion, and publicity purposes without further compensation to or permission from the entrants, except where prohibited by law.

8. By participating in this sweepstakes, entrants agree to be bound by these rules and the decisions of the judges and sweepstakes sponsors, which are final in all matters relating to the sweepstakes.

9. For a list of major prizewinners (available after 7/15/98), send a stamped, self-addressed envelope to Prizewinners, Pocket Books/Sabrina, The Teenage Witch Sweepstakes, 13th Floor, 1230 Avenue of the Americas, NY, NY 10020.

10. Simon & Schuster is the official sweepstakes sponsor.

11. The sweepstakes sponsors shall have no liability for any injury, loss, or damage of any kind arising out of participation in this sweepstakes or the acceptance or use of the prize. Viacom Productions, Paramount Pictures, and Archie Comic Publications, Inc., and their respective parent and affiliated companies are not responsible for fulfillment of prizes or for any loss, damage, or injury suffered as a result of the set tour or use or acceptance of prizes.

™ Archie Comic Publications, Inc. © 1997 Viacom Productions, Inc. All Rights Reserved.

Official Entry Form

Name _____

Address _____

City _____ State _____ Zip _____

Phone _____